the **BAD GUYS**

in

OPEN WIDE
AND
SAY ARRRGH!

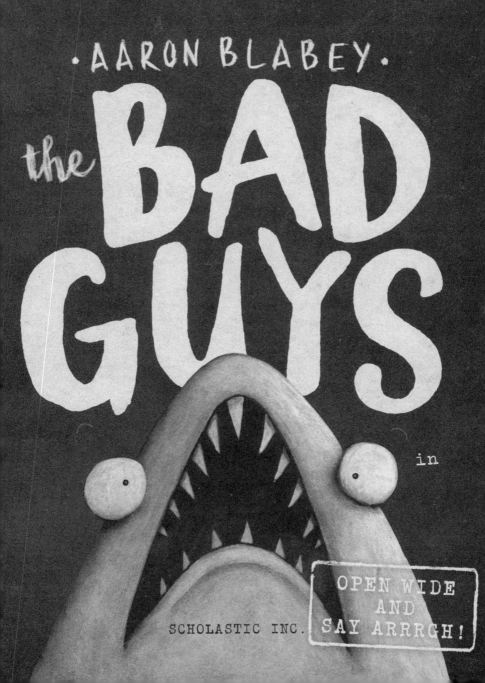

· AARON BLABEY ·

the BAD GUYS

in

OPEN WIDE
AND
SAY ARRRGH!

SCHOLASTIC INC.

Pssst!

Hey, Wolfie . . .

I don't know. Is this bad? This seems kind of . . .
Fun, right?
I guess . . . But I think I'd better get—

I have my momennnnnnngghh . . .
MOMENNNNNGGHH . . .
MOMENNNNGGHHHH
I'M SORRY . . . WHAT DID YOU SAY?

· CHAPTER 1 ·

THE DENTAL APPOINTMENT

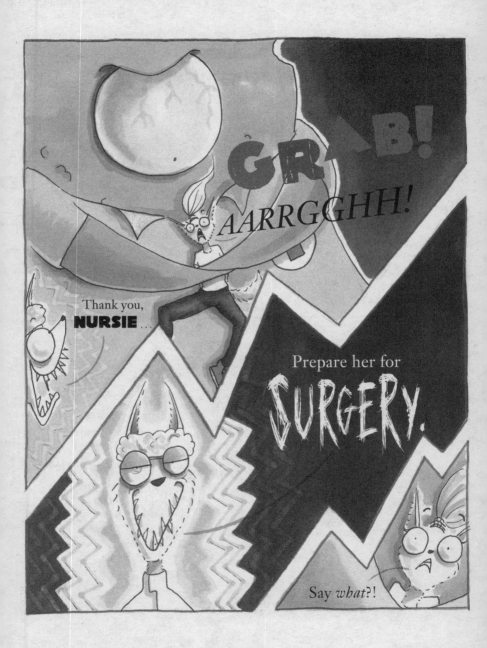

LETMEGO! GETOFFME!

ISN'T THIS A BLAST?!

MMMM!

Look, I'm just gonna say it . . . your conversation skills kind of **STINK**, you know?

MMM MMM!

No, no. STOP. You're just embarrassing yourself. I'll take it from here.

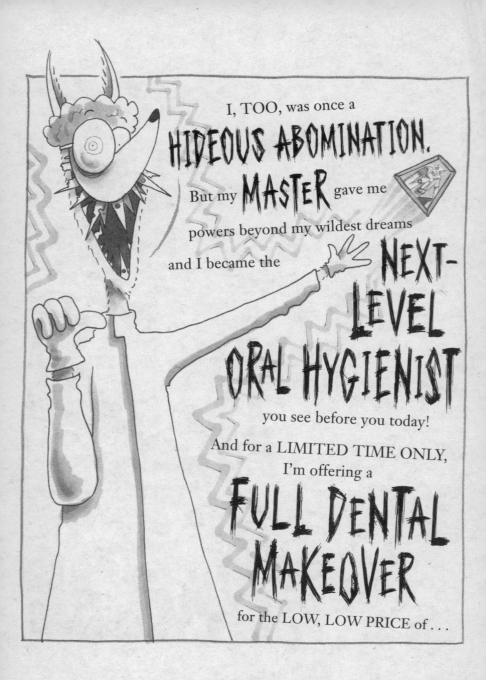

I, TOO, was once a **HIDEOUS ABOMINATION.** But my **MASTER** gave me powers beyond my wildest dreams and I became the **NEXT-LEVEL ORAL HYGIENIST** you see before you today! And for a LIMITED TIME ONLY, I'm offering a **FULL DENTAL MAKEOVER** for the LOW, LOW PRICE of . . .

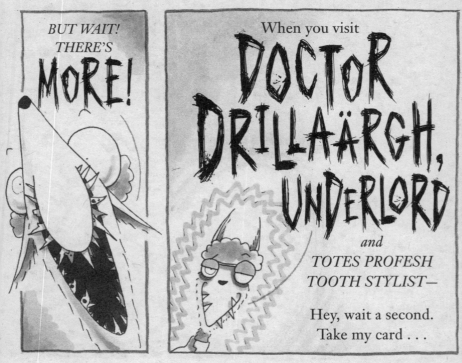

DR. DAVID DRILLAÄRGH

Amateur Dental Surgery Enthusiast

"Hey, who needs a diploma?"

When you visit me,
you don't get boring old

HAPPY GAS

and itty-bitty

DRILL BITS!

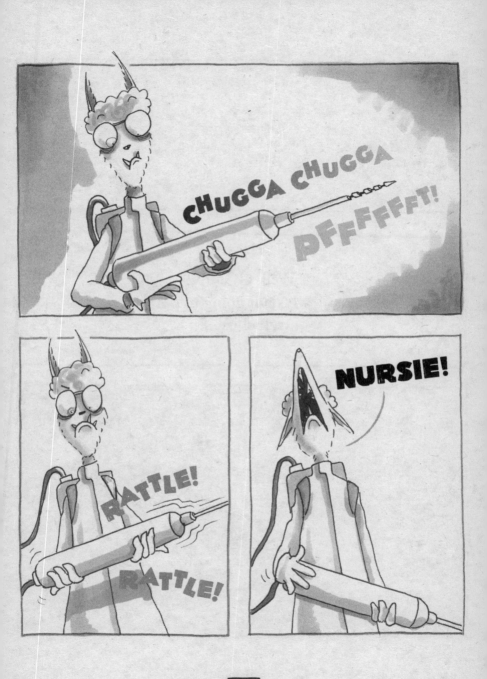

Lollipop?

The only thing we have going for us is the **ELEMENT OF SURPRISE.**

If **SNAKE** sees us coming, we're done for. And **FOX** isn't here to help us this time.

If he gets us, we're *his*.

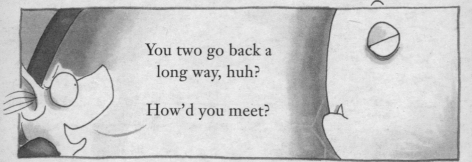

I was eating out one night . . .

. . . when this little guy came out of nowhere
and started screaming that I'd stolen his meal.

I informed him that he was mistaken.

CRUNCH!

He considered this for a moment
. . . and then said,

"Sure, *chico*. You have
that little entrée.
You've put me in the
mood for . . ."

A MAIN COURSE.

What a beautiful story.

**HEY, LOOK!
IS THAT . . . ?**

IT'S HIM!

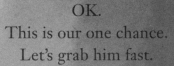

OK.
This is our one chance.
Let's grab him fast.

And don't forget, this is
all about the element of . . .

· CHAPTER 3 ·
THE UTENSIL WITHIN

Breathe, Fluffit.

How often do you get to watch a

VELOCIRAPTOR

have a conversation with a

CHAIN SAW MANIAC?

IN SPACE?!

This is compelling stuff.

MILT!

SHOW ME...

He's not as scary as he seems!
He's not some unbeatable MONSTER.
He just **LOOKED** like one.

It's like SNAKE.
Underneath, *on the inside*,
he's just plain old Snake.

We can BEAT these guys!

All we have to do is
NOT BE AFRAID
of them.

Hold up.

If any of **US** tried what the dinosaur

just did, we'd be *dead*.

We wouldn't have even made it outside the ship.

And even if we *did* survive being

CRUSHED BY SPACE,

we'd have been

CHOPPED
TO PIECES.

What just happened didn't

make any sense.

We should

TOTALLY

be afraid of them.

· CHAPTER 4 ·
DARK AND WEIRD

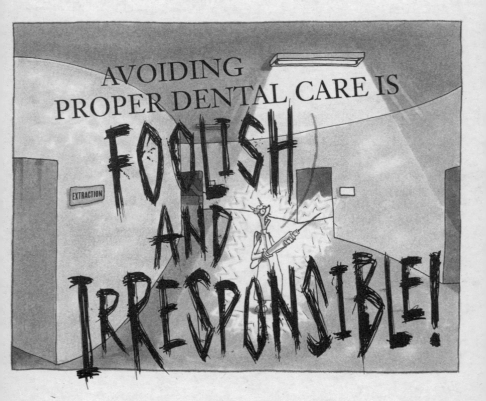

If our **LIFE WAS A SERIES**, you would say it was getting WEIRD and DARK.

Like, a lot weirder and darker than those highly accessible early books . . .

It's because we're getting close to . . . *you know who.*

The **HEAVY METAL CENTIPEDE?**

I'm a **BAT**.

And sorry—full disclosure—I was

EAVESDROPPING.

I heard everything you said.

Did you say you know where **THE DOORWAY** is?

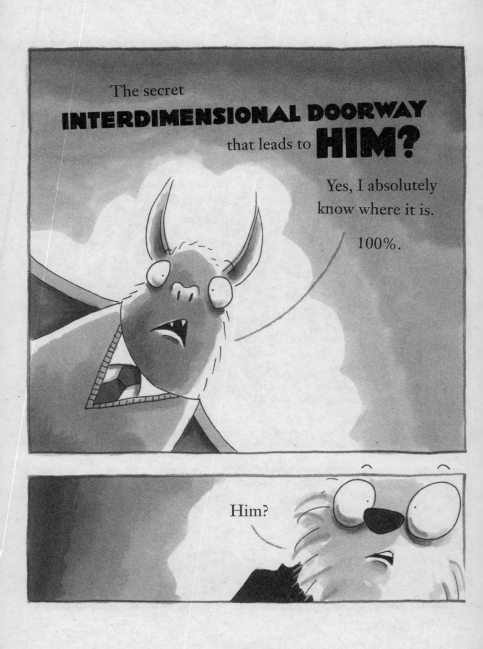

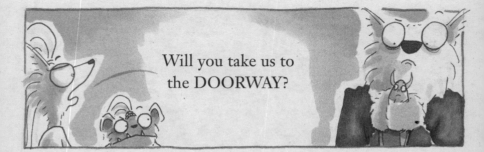

Will you take us to the DOORWAY?

Yes, of course.

But it IS a bit **INCONVENIENT** because I'm supposed to be doing **SOMETHING ELSE**.

I'm not trying to make you feel guilty. I just can't hide my feelings and I feel compelled to share them.

Can't help it.

I'm pathologically honest and . . .

WHAT were you supposed to be doing? Instead of taking us to **THE DOORWAY?**

I'm supposed to wait until **THE ONE** arrives.

CHAPTER 5

WHO NEEDS MAGIC HANDS?

CHICOS!
GET OUT
OF HERE!

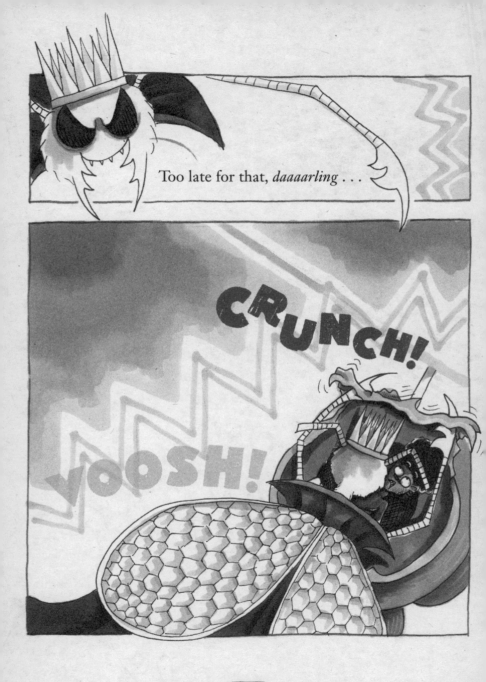

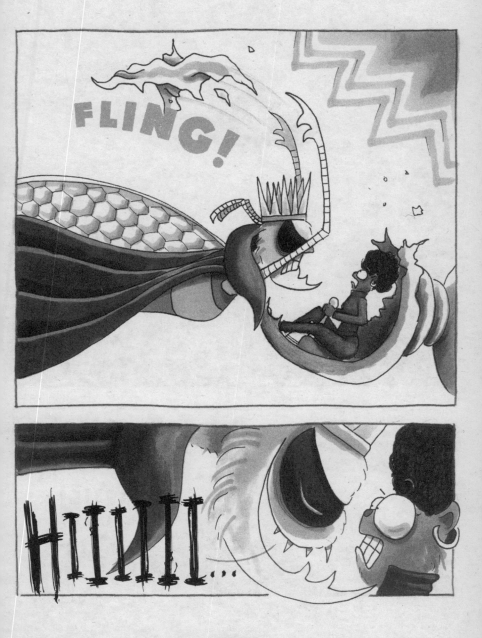

You guys are SO predictable, you know that?

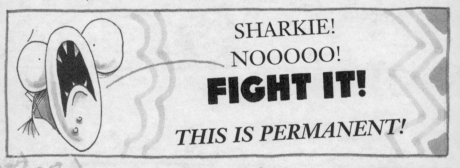

· CHAPTER 6 ·
IMPORTANT HOW?

And there goes **DICKIE,** the **INTERGALACTIC BABY SPOON.**

If anyone needed proof this is a less important subplot, *there it goes . . .*

WRONG!

· CHAPTER 7 ·
THE TRUTH TELLER

· CHAPTER 8 ·
ONE AT A TIME, PLEASE

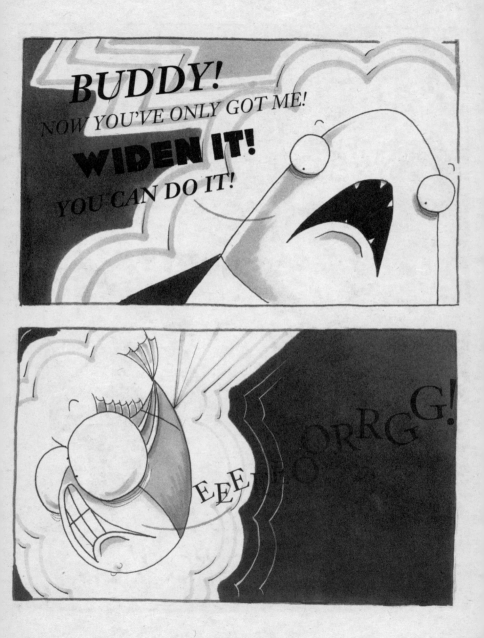

DON'T YOU DO IT, PIRANHA!
KITTY, BABY, THIS MAKES SENSE . . .
IT DOES!
NO!
WE'LL BE OK. SOMEHOW . . . SOMEDAY . . .
IT'LL ALL BE OK IN THE END . . .

· CHAPTER 9 ·
THE OTHERS

This is the place?

Where are they?

Buck?!

Oh, quit yo' fussin' . . .

Well, I ain't here
for a haircut.

But where are the others?
I mean the *other* OTHERS?
Where are the rest of you?

What's wrong with you, gal?
He's **RIGHT THERE**.

There are **FOUR**.

There's me, **ZEE**.

There's **GRANNY GUMBO JUMBO**.

There's **HONEST ABE**. Out there, all alone somewhere . . .

· CHAPTER 10 ·
ABE IN THE WOODS

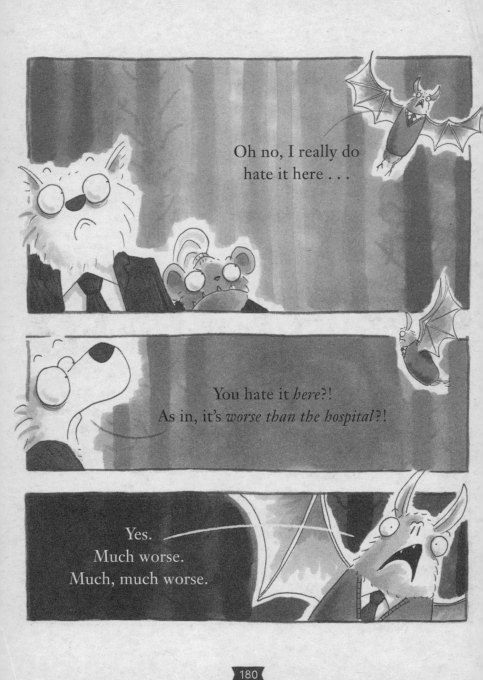

Oh, she's **BAD**.
And when she's around,
everything turns bad.

Wonderful.

Do you know where the
next Doorway is?